My Other Life

Polly Ho-Yen

Illustrated by Patricia Hu

BLOOMSBURY EDUCATION

BLOOMSBURY EDUCATION
Bloomsbury Publishing Plc
50 Bedford Square, London, WC1B 3DP, UK

BLOOMSBURY, BLOOMSBURY EDUCATION and the Diana logo
are trademarks of Bloomsbury Publishing Plc

First published in 2020 by Bloomsbury Publishing Plc

Packaged for Bloomsbury by Plum5 Limited

A catalogue record for this book is available from the British Library

ISBN: PB 978-1-4729-7257-6;
ePDF: 978-1-4729-7256-9; ePub: 978-1-4729-7258-3

2 4 6 8 10 9 7 5 3 1

Printed and bound by CPI Group (UK) Ltd, Croydon, CR20 4YY

Contents

The Hole in the Hospital

I was in hospital when I saw the first hole.

I've spent quite a lot of time in hospital.

When I was quite young, I was diagnosed with severe asthma and if I get a bad attack, I often end up there. My mum says that we've had some "near brushes" which always makes me think of my old hairbrush, clogged up with tangles and dull, dead hair.

I can't remember properly the times I was unwell. My dad says I'm the bravest person he knows, but I don't know what he means by that.

My friend Rav says: "Mae, I think you're the greatest. And your dad makes the best lunches." I say: "Is that why you like me, because I have the best lunches – and I always give them to you?" He laughs and says: "Of course not," but then he rubs his belly as he says it. I don't think he even notices he's doing it.

My asthma's not a big deal. Not really. And it's got better now I am older and understand what I need to do. I know that I have to take my medicine every day. And I know that I have to get help if I feel a tightening in my chest, or a wheeze in my breath. And I also know that, unless I grow out of it, I will have to do this for the rest of my life.

I don't like being in hospital. It's always just a bit too hot for one thing. When I get home after being there, the first thing I do is open up my bedroom window, as wide as it can go, and I leave it like that, all night if Mum doesn't notice, so I can feel the breeze coming in and all around me. Sometimes, when I'm just dropping off to sleep, it makes me feel like I'm floating off my bed, the cold crisp air lifting me up, up and away.

But the very first time I saw the hole was when I was in hospital.

I'd caught some kind of chest infection and I was having difficulty breathing. My inhalers hadn't made it any better, so Mum said we should go there right away.

It had been a while since my last visit. Dad was away seeing Grandma for the night and so it was just Mum and me. She called an ambulance and though it came pretty quickly, I could tell she was getting worried; her large dark eyes glazed over with concern each time she looked at me.

As soon as I was in the ambulance, they started me on oxygen and when we arrived at the hospital we got taken to a small room with a large window that looked down on the road below.

A nurse had just woken me to check my levels and, as she left, Mum asked me if I was feeling any better. I said I thought I was, although I could still feel the tightness in my chest. I looked away from her, towards the door that the nurse had just left through.

And that's when I saw it.

The hole.

It was just a tiny sliver of space, which for a few moments – there are no other words for it – opened up.

In the hole there were masses and masses of tiny black lines; loads and loads of lines all muddled together like someone had taken a black pen to a piece of paper and scribbled and scribbled and scribbled, so there was almost no white left there at all.

"What is it?" I blurted out. "What's that?"

"Mae!" Mum reached for my hand. "Are you all right?"

"There, by the door!" I sat upright.

But as I pointed towards it, I could see the gap knit itself back together as though it had never existed. The black squiggles vanished completely. It was like there had been a tear in some fabric and now the two torn edges had been stitched back together, making it as good as new. It was just an ordinary room again.

"What is it, Mae?" Mum looked worried and white, and turned towards the space that I was gesturing at, which now looked like just what it was: an empty space by a boring old hospital door.

"I thought I saw..." I started to say but I didn't know how to explain it, so I lay back again, feeling completely exhausted, like I could sleep for a hundred years if anyone would let me.

"I'll get the nurse," Mum said, sweeping my fringe away and holding her hand to my forehead.

"Don't go," I said, but I could feel myself drifting away from her under the waves of sleep.

"I'll be right back," she said, planting a kiss on my head. Then I heard the sound of her footsteps running out of the room.

But I managed to keep my eyes open just long enough for me to see that, as she ran past the place where the gap had appeared, nothing out of the ordinary happened.

It was as though the hole had never been there.

The Second Hole

"There she is!" Dad said, ruffling my hair with one hand and squeezing my arm with the other.

He'd driven through the night from Grandma's, and so when I woke up the next morning, he was the first thing I saw as I opened my eyes.

It took me a few moments to remember that I was in hospital, but then I took it all in: the funny antiseptic smell, the green walls that were so different to the yellow ones of my bedroom.

A doctor had come to see us and told Mum and Dad that they would monitor how I was doing, but I wouldn't be able to go home today if my oxygen levels didn't go up.

"Well, that's that," Mum said when the doctor left, and then she sat back in her chair; she almost seemed to sink into its shiny fabric and become part of the seat. Dad reached out and rested his hand on Mum's head gently. She looked at him gratefully and then reached her hand up to his so they could lock fingers.

"Are you OK?" he asked her in a quiet voice.

Mum nodded slowly and just at that moment, behind where Dad

was standing, I saw the second
hole appear.

This hole grew bigger, in bursts,
with each nod of Mum's head. For a
moment I was worried that the hole
would grow so large it would swallow
up the whole room and all of us in it.

I sat up in alarm.

"What is it, darling?" I heard
Mum say.

"Are you OK, Mae?" Dad
said. "We're right here, pet. We're
right here."

And then, as quickly as it had
appeared, the hole folded in on itself
and disappeared completely.

Rav's Theory

"What do you mean – a hole?" Rav said. He was picking his nose with a squinted look of concentration.

"I mean exactly what I said – a hole. Like a hole in the world."

"Like a crater?" Rav said, finger still fully inserted into his nostril.

It was disgusting behaviour, but I suppose it sort of showed why I felt able to tell Rav what I'd seen in hospital. We're not the kind of best friends that fall out and then become friends again and fall out again and then have another best friend. We've stuck together since the first day of primary school when we met.

And we've always felt able to be completely ourselves with each other. I don't have to put on a show for Rav; I can just be me, quiet little me, who has to go to hospital a lot, and Rav accepts me and likes me just how I am. And I put up with his nose-picking, and him always wanting my lunch, and a whole array of other Rav-specific things, and we're friends. It's just the way it's always been.

"No, not a crater. It was in the hospital room and it was there one minute and then gone the next."

"And you definitely didn't imagine it. Did they give you some powerful drugs? My sister said she could see all kinds of things when they gave her something for the pain, when she had her appendix out. Like little goblins coming out of the ceiling that were eating their own ears. It's true – ask her."

"No, it wasn't like that. I wasn't delirious. Or seeing things. I know it sounds weird. But it's like there was something behind this –" I waved my hand around me. We were sitting on one of the benches in the corner of the playground; kids kept running past us in a swirl of noise and screams – "like this was just fabric and behind it there were lines, all kinds of scribbly black lines," I tried to explain.

"Like to another world or something?" Rav asked. "Like a portal?" Rav is very keen on video games that have portals in them.

"Yeah – more like that," I said. "More like a portal."

"Well, in that case," Rav said, "you've got to find out what's on the other side. If it's a portal, then it will lead somewhere else."

"Somewhere else?"

"Yeah – like sometimes it could just be a different place in this world or it could be, well – anywhere... Got it!"

Rav removed his finger with a flourish and flicked the bogey across the playground an impressive distance.

"You really are disgusting, d'you know that?" I said.

"But you're the one who's crazy — seeing portals," Rav said back with a grin.

"Hmm. Well, maybe I won't see any more."

"Maybe it's something to do with the hospital. Have you seen one anywhere else?" he asked.

"No. Only in hospital, only those two."

"Well, that might be it then," Rav said cheerfully. "So don't worry about it too much."

"I'm not worried..." I started to say, but Rav was already laughing at me, his shoulders shaking.

"I'm not worried," he mimicked, screwing up his forehead into a big furrow.

And I knew he was right. I was worried about it and I was also sure that I didn't want to see another hole. I couldn't tell you why exactly, only that I was hoping, hoping with every bit of me, that that would be the end of it completely.

The Centre of the Hole

Six months went by and life went back to normal. Dad went to visit Grandma almost every weekend, and we often went with him.

I started to feel a bit wheezy on one of our visits to her, but I recovered pretty quickly when I used my inhalers, so we didn't have to go to hospital or anything like that.

To be honest, I found the trips to Grandma's quite boring, although the only person I would admit that to was Rav. It was a long car journey and then when we got there we spent the whole time in Grandma's little sitting room, which was just a bit too small when all of us were in it.

We always talked about the same things over and over – the time when they used to live in Guyana when Dad was a small boy and Grandma was a nurse and about people who I'd never met – Grandma's brother who had the funny nickname of Chewie and wore his hair in a big quiff and her best friend Jeannie who had died the year before.

Mum said we needed to appreciate the time we had with Grandma and with each other, but I found it hard to do that when I was there. I spent most of the time staring at the dust balls in the carpet or at the shelf of funny little china ornaments that I wasn't allowed to touch in case I broke them, counting down the minutes until Dad would slap his hands on his knees and say, "Afraid we've got to hit the road, Mum."

Then I'd kiss Grandma on her thin cheek gently and in that moment I would be able to smell the fresh scent of soap on her skin and would feel, oddly, even though I'd been bored stiff for the last two hours, that I didn't want to leave her.

One Saturday morning though, when we were packing up the car to go and celebrate Grandma's birthday, which had been earlier in the week, I felt the familiar gripping around my lungs and my breath started to come in short, sharp gasps.

Mum noticed straightaway.

"Are you all right, Mae?" she asked.

I tried to say "my inhaler" but it was too hard to speak and breathe at the same time. Before I knew it, Dad was in front of me in a flash with the nebulizer I have to use.

"Take it slowly," he said, his eyes warm and steady on mine.

I gave him the tiniest of nods.

"That's it – nice and slow, Mae," Mum said, kneeling down so she was right next to me. Her hand reached for mine and I squeezed it tightly.

Dad had been cooking the night before to make some of the special dishes that they used to eat in Guyana. He'd packed two huge bags of food into the boot of the car; I could just make out the outline of the bags beyond us.

"Well done, Mae," Dad said. "You're doing so well. Just keep breathing nice and slow, like we practised."

I felt Mum squeeze my hand. "That's it, darling," she whispered.

I closed my eyes to concentrate on my breathing, but even with my eyes shut I could feel and sense how close my parents were next to me. It felt like we made a triangle, and each of us was one of its points.

"How's that now?" Dad asked. I shook my head a little to tell him it wasn't helping and without me having to say a word, Mum rang for an ambulance while Dad lifted me up and back into the house.

They laid me down on the sofa and once they'd made me comfortable, Mum dashed upstairs to pack a bag for hospital and Dad went to find my other inhalers.

Suddenly, in those brief moments while they left my side, another hole split open, right in front of me.

It started small, just a little tear, but I could tell at once from the way it grew and swelled that it would become even bigger than the other two I'd seen.

The scribbly black lines swarmed. They made my chest grow tighter when I looked at them. They were constantly moving and entangling with one another, like thousands and thousands of headless snakes writhing in a heap.

This time the hole had opened close enough to me that I could touch it. I remembered what Rav had said about portals: that they had to lead somewhere. I reached one hand towards the black swirling mass.

I could hear the sound of Dad's footsteps running back down the stairs and Mum clunking drawers shut in my bedroom.

My fingers stroked the air in front of the hole and then with one final push I found myself reaching through the black lines, and as the very tips of my fingers disappeared through the hole, I felt my whole body being pulled towards it.

And though it was my movement of reaching forward, it felt like I had no control to stop myself. Before I knew what was happening, I was being drawn into the twirling chaos of the lines, and sucked right into its centre.

No One There

It felt like I was underwater.

I was sure I could not breathe.

The black lines were so thick around me, they were pressing in on me, almost crushing me. But just as I was beginning to panic, I was suddenly released.

I opened my eyes and took in a deep breath.

I was exactly where I had been before – lying on the sofa in the sitting room.

I laughed out loud when I saw that nothing had happened; I hadn't gone anywhere; the hole wasn't a portal after all.

I touched the space in the air where the hole had been but like the last time it had stitched itself up and there was no trace of it any more.

Then I noticed that two things had changed: I could no longer hear the sounds of Mum and Dad, and the gripping, coiling feeling that I'd held inside my chest had lifted. My breath came easily once again, and the pain in my lungs that I'd felt was closing in on me had receded so far I couldn't even think what it had felt like.

For a moment I stayed on the sofa and listened a little more closely, but when the house remained silent

I swung my legs from the sofa and padded upstairs.

There was no one there.

Mum and Dad

Had I passed out and had they left the house for some reason? It seemed unlikely as we were waiting for the ambulance to arrive.

Perhaps they were waiting outside? But when I opened the front door, there was no sign of them there either.

I shouted out for them, even though I knew they weren't there.

I tried calling them on their mobiles but there was no answer. Part of me wanted to go and look for them but I didn't want to leave the house in case they came back. I decided to message Rav, to tell him what had happened, but when I tried to do it, his number had gone from my phone. It had been playing up a bit recently, shutting down by itself and freezing sometimes, so I didn't think it was odd, I thought it was something to do with that.

As I walked around the house, I noticed that some things were missing – the picture on the wall of us in Grandma's garden last year, the paintings that I'd made for Mum for her birthday. I couldn't understand why they had been replaced with a bland picture of the sea and a sign that read: "Home Is Where the Heart Is".

I sat on my bed and waited, wishing for them to be there and for things to feel normal again.

When Mum and Dad finally walked through the door a couple of hours later, they acted like nothing had happened, although they were perhaps a bit quieter than usual. They looked a little pale and tired, I thought.

I had run down the stairs when I heard the front door opening and almost collided with Dad.

"Where were you?" I demanded.

"What do you mean?" he said.

"We told you when we left this morning – we were at the conference."

"Conference?"

Mum yawned loudly. "I didn't think it was ever going to finish."

"What about the ambulance?" I said.

"What ambulance?" Dad asked. He glanced out of the window. "Did you see one on the road? It might have been for Ivy. I haven't seen her out and about for a little while. I wonder if she's had a turn for the worse."

"No, for me!" I exclaimed.

"What are you talking about, Mae?"

"I was having an asthma attack."
I couldn't understand why they were
pretending they didn't know what
was happening, and what was this
conference they were talking about?

"Asthma attack!" Mum scoffed
and looked over at Dad with raised
eyebrows. "I don't know where she
gets this stuff from."

"It's true," I said desperately.

"Did something happen while
we were out?" Dad asked. "And you
called an ambulance?"

"You were there... you called the
ambulance. We were going to see
Grandma, for her birthday."

Mum and Dad exchanged a look with raised eyebrows.

"Mae," Mum said with a deep breath. "I don't know why you would be making this up, I really don't, but your father and I have had a long day. We're very tired and we're not in the mood to play one of your games right now, OK?"

I opened my mouth to say that I wasn't making it up, that I was worried about where they'd disappeared to, but the looks on their faces silenced me. Without saying another word, I turned my back on them and ran up to my bedroom, burying my head in my pillow as though I could block everything out.

When Mum came up a bit later, she didn't mention the conversation we'd had, she just said that dinner was ready. When I came down I saw there were takeaway boxes in the kitchen and Dad said to help myself. It seemed like a peace offering as we only ever have takeaways as a treat. I wasn't hungry but I spooned a little food on to a plate. When I went through to the dining room, I saw that the table was covered with paperwork I'd never seen before, so Mum and Dad were eating on the sofa with the television on. They had the same white tiredness on their faces that they had when they walked in; no one spoke very much.

I went to bed early in the end but I lay awake for hours, trying to unpick what it was that was different and why things felt so changed.

Rav

The next day at school, I waited for Rav in the corner of the playground by the big bristly bush where we'd always meet if both of us were in. I felt desperate to speak to him. Mum and Dad were still acting a bit strangely at breakfast time.

Dad had said, "The less said about yesterday, the better, OK?" I didn't know why he was saying that, but I just nodded and quietly ate the cereal in my bowl.

And there was another slightly weird thing that happened. Neither Mum nor Dad bothered to check if I had taken my daily inhalers.

Usually one or even both of them make sure I've done it. But Dad had gone for a shower and Mum had said she needed to get to work early and rushed off before I'd finished eating.

I looked in the kitchen cupboard where we keep the inhalers but they weren't there. I breathed in and out. My breath came clear and strong, and because Dad was still in the shower, I thought I'd ask later where they'd moved them to and hoped I wouldn't need them today.

While I was sitting waiting by the bush, I spotted Rav standing across the playground talking to some people in the other class. I made my way over to him.

"Hey," I said.

He looked at me. "Hey."

I stood next to him and the two boys he was with. They started talking about something I hadn't heard of, as if I wasn't there.

"Rav?" I tried again.

"Umm... yeah?"

"Can I talk to you?" I asked.

He looked at the ground and then back to the two boys, who were staring at me like there was something on my face.

"What is it?" he asked.

"Over here," I said impatiently and tugged at his arm.

He struggled out of my grip but followed me over.

"What is it?" he said again.

"I just need to talk to you," I said. "I need to speak to a friend right now."

Then Rav's face changed. It wasn't unkind, really, or mean – he just seemed sort of startled, surprised, kind of troubled. He looked at me with narrowed eyes.

"We don't talk," he said. "We're not friends."

I couldn't stop the tears that were suddenly gathering in my eyes.

"What did I do? Why are you behaving like this?"

"What do you mean?" he asked.

"Is it because of what I said on Friday? About you being greedy. I didn't mean it. You know I didn't. I mean you always eat my lunch, but I don't mind. Look – have something now, what have we got today...?" I delved into my school bag, reaching for the packed lunch that Dad always makes for me, but found it was empty. There was nothing there.

"What are you talking about?" Rav said. "I never eat your lunch."

I couldn't stop laughing then, out of relief if nothing else. He was joking; it was all just a stupid joke.

"Sorry," I said and held my hands up. "You're right." I tried to keep a straight face. "You never touch my food. Well, that's a good thing, because Dad forgot to put anything in my bag today."

I felt my hand reaching for Rav's arm, as though I wanted to make sure he was solid.

"Sorry," Rav said, taking a step away from me as he spoke. "But I really don't know what you're talking about."

And then he just turned and walked away.

Mandy

I spent all day in what felt like a kind of fog. I couldn't quite tell where my feet were or what was ahead of me.

Just after Rav stalked off, a girl called Mandy, who I'd never spent much time with before, ran up to me and reached for my hand, squeezing it tightly.

"What were you talking to him for?" she said, looking at Rav through narrowed eyes. It wasn't a nice look.

Before I could respond she leaned into me closely.

"So did you do it?" she asked.

"What?" I said.

She rolled her eyes. "Did you tell them?"

"Tell them... tell them what? Who do you mean?"

"Mae! Stop being funny!" Mandy said. She gave a tinkling little laugh.

"I don't know what you're talking about."

"Stop it! Be serious."

"Um..."

Mandy's eyes started to narrow again and flashed darker. "You didn't, did you. I knew you didn't have it in you."

"It didn't seem like the right time," I said vaguely. Mandy frowned and she dropped my hand.

"We were going to see Grandma for her birthday," I said. "And then I started to get an asthma attack. I thought I was going to have to go to hospital again."

"What do you mean again?" Mandy demanded.

"You know – I have to go to hospital when my asthma gets bad."

"You've never been to hospital the whole time I've known you and you don't have asthma. What are you talking about?"

"How long have I known you?"

Mandy laughed again. But this time it sounded much more brittle.

"Seriously, how long have we known each other, how long have we been... friends?" I asked.

"Stop being so weird, Mae. It's not funny any more. I've known you since the start of school."

'We met on the first day of school..." I said slowly.

"Yeah – we've always been friends, since the very first day," Mandy said.

"Just like Rav," I murmured. I looked over to where he was still talking to the two boys. He was standing in between them and looked like he was telling a joke. I thought I saw him looking over at me. I smiled hopefully but he turned away.

"What did you say?" Mandy spluttered.

"I mean… and we tell each other everything," I said quickly.

"Yes," Mandy said, looping her arm in mine. "You tell me everything."

"And I haven't always been in and out of hospital. And I don't have asthma."

Mandy looked at me strangely and dropped my arm.

"I'm not going to talk to you if you keep being weird," she said.

Then she walked away and I was left standing alone in the playground.

I could still see Rav in the corner
of my eye but he didn't look over at
me again.

Another Place

Rav, the real Rav, had been right: the hole was a portal to another place. I had come to a place where I didn't have asthma. Where I never had to worry about getting an attack, where my mum and dad didn't have to be concerned or even think about it.

I had come to a place which, if I was being honest with myself, I had sometimes wished for. There had been some brief moments when I had wondered what my life would be like if I'd been born being able to breathe as easily as most other people.

But this was nothing like I had hoped it would be.

I had come through the hole to a place where I couldn't speak to anyone, not properly. Where I couldn't be myself. Not with Rav. Definitely not with Mandy. Not even with Mum and Dad.

The Surprise

We were eating dinner in front of the television again, another takeaway. I never thought I'd say this, but I was starting to get a little bored of the taste of takeaways. I craved one of Dad's home-cooked meals. But it didn't seem like this dad cooked like he did in my real home. When I looked in the kitchen cupboards, there were none of the sauces and spices that my real dad used.

Since I had realised where I was, I'd seen even more differences in our house. It was a lot tidier than my real home. A cleaner came every week, here.

I'd noticed other things that were missing too: the scuffed pencil marks on the wall showing how tall I'd grown each year, the grease stain on the kitchen ceiling from where Dad had tossed a pancake too high.

I glanced across at my other parents. They looked just like my real mum and dad, but there was something very different about them. They were with me, but sometimes it felt as though they didn't even know I was there.

I pushed the red curry sauce around my plate. It seemed more and more unappetizing the more I looked at it. Mum and Dad stared at the television, pushing forkfuls of food into their open mouths.

"I'm full now," I said and stood up to take my plate to the kitchen.

"Hang on a tick, Mae. We've got something to tell you," said Mum.

I turned round, surprised. They were both slumped across the sofa but there was something that lit up their eyes a little.

"What is it?" I asked.

"We're moving!" Dad said triumphantly, slapping his hands on his thighs as he said it, so his plate wobbled and almost fell off his lap.

"Moving? Moving where?"

"Not too far away," Mum said quickly. "But it's a massive house; there's loads more space. A lovely big kitchen, a much bigger garden, you're going to love it!" She started tapping on her phone and then passed it over to me so I could see the photos.

"We didn't want to get your hopes up before we knew it was going to go ahead," said Dad. "But work's going really well, we've had the mortgage approved and now it's go, go, go."

"We know you don't like how small your room is," Mum added. "In the new house, your room is huge! You'll be able to have Mandy round for sleepovers and just have more space to spread out."

I looked at their glowing faces, dumbfounded. I couldn't imagine living anywhere other than the house we'd lived in for my entire life and I love my bedroom, I don't think I've ever said it was too small.

I looked again through the photos of the large rooms of the new house. Suddenly, an email popped up on the screen, so I passed the phone back to Mum.

It struck me that in this reality I didn't know what Mum and Dad did for work, apart from them saying they'd been to a conference. In the old place, Mum worked part-time at a doctor's surgery as a receptionist and Dad did freelance carpentry work.

We didn't have loads of money but that didn't seem to bother us.

"You're going to love it!" Mum said again, but when I looked up at her she wasn't looking at me any more, she was scrolling through her phone.

"Um... can I go to see it?" I asked.

"Of course," Dad said. "But not for a few days. Your mother and I are going away. We're off to check on some new suppliers tomorrow and then we have meetings out of town for most of next week."

"We're not going to visit Grandma this weekend?" I asked.

"We'll see her at Christmas,"
Dad said.

"But that's months away..." I began.

"Mae," Mum said in a warning
tone. "You're going to stay with
Mandy over the weekend and then
Tracey's got space for you next week
while we're away. But when we get
back, we'll go to see the new house."

"Who's Tracey?"

"Don't be silly, Mae," Mum said
shortly. "It doesn't suit you."

I felt her words like cuts; they
stung.

Mum looked at me appraisingly.
"Aren't you excited about the house?"

she said. "You've been talking about wanting to move for so long."

"Yes, I'm pleased," I lied.

"I thought you'd be happier," she said. She sounded sad but when I looked up again, she was still staring at her phone.

Mandy's House

Mandy did not look happy to see us when Mum walked me up to their front door the next morning. It was still quite early but Mum said they needed to get on the road as soon as they could. I'd looked at some papers they had left lying about and found out that they both worked for a drinks company, something to do with marketing.

"Hello, Mae, come on in," Mandy's mother said to me in place of Mandy saying anything. Mandy just stared at me.

Mum handed over my bag and I stepped inside. I could hear Mandy's mum mouth to my mum, "She'll be fine," over my head.

Mandy's house was huge. I stood in the hallway, which was bigger than our kitchen and sitting room put together, not sure where to go or what to do with myself. Mandy darted up the stairs before I could follow.

"Why don't you take your bag upstairs?" her mum said as we both watched her disappear. "She's in one of her moods I'm afraid, but I know she's excited you're staying over."

I struggled up the wide staircase, unsure of where I was going and wondering whether there was any part of me or Mandy that was excited we were spending the weekend together.

Time passed tediously and slowly. I knew, before I even opened my mouth, that whatever I said would not be the sort of thing that Mandy wanted to hear. She wanted to spend a long time reading magazines and wanted to comment – and me to comment – on every celebrity on each page.

"What do you think of her?" She pointed to someone on the red carpet. "What do you think of her clothes?"

I had no interest in it, but I looked over.

"I don't think that dress works for her," Mandy said definitively.

"I... I... don't care."

"What's wrong with you?" she snapped.

"Nothing's wrong with me."

"Why are you behaving so weirdly?"

"Maybe because I'm weird."

Mandy snorted. "You've got that right."

"And I'm having a weird time."

"What's going on?" Mandy asked, a little more gently.

For a moment I struggled to know where to start. Could I tell her about the portal and all that had changed?

"My mum and dad want to move house," I blurted out in the end.

"Will you have a bigger bedroom?" Mandy asked.

"Yes."

"Well, what's wrong then, Mae? That's everything you ever wanted! You're always saying how jealous you are of our house and my bedroom and everything. I said you needed to tell them you couldn't go on living there like that."

"That was what you wanted me to tell them?"

"You wanted to tell them! You were going to say you would run away if you didn't move to a bigger house."

"D-did I say that?" I stuttered.

"It's important to you," Mandy said with a shrug before turning another page of the magazine. "OK, tell me honestly... isn't this the worst hairstyle you've ever seen?"

The Fourth Hole

It turned out Tracey was a childminder that I would often go and stay with when Mum and Dad were working away from home. The week with her passed slowly but it was better than being at Mandy's.

When Mum and Dad arrived to pick me up, I was so glad to see them that I couldn't stop myself from running to them for a hug, but just as their arms closed around me, Mum's phone started ringing and she had to break off.

"Give me a minute," she said.

"Had a good week, Mae?" Dad asked.

I shrugged but he didn't seem to notice.

"Good, good."

"Right, that's all done and dusted," Mum said finally. "Let's go."

When we were all in the car, I plucked up the courage to speak.

"Mum, Dad, can I speak to you about something?"

"Can it wait until later?" Mum said.

"Um, I guess so."

"Great, I just need to send some emails before we get there."

"Get where?"

"We're going to stop off at the new house on our way home. We can't wait for you to see it."

The new house was, as Mum and Dad said, much, much bigger. It was brand new and so it didn't have any furniture in it, which made the wide-open spaces seem even vaster.

"This will be your room," Mum said, leading me into a huge cavernous room that had large windows looking out on to the garden below.

"Do you like it?" Dad asked. "Is it big enough?"

I made a non-committal kind of noise. I took a deep breath. "Can I talk to you about Grandma?"

Mum strode off towards the window and said, "What's there to talk about? Just look at that view, won't you?"

I'd wanted to ask them if we could go and see her. I missed being there. I missed being there together. I thought that perhaps if we went there, this mum and dad might stop for a moment and talk, like we do in my real home. That was what was different about this mum and dad, they were always on the go, they couldn't concentrate on me long enough for us to talk properly.

One of their phones bleeped. The message that came through meant they needed to make a phone call urgently so they left me there in my new room. I imagined where my bed might be and sat in that space, on the new carpet that sunk thickly beneath me.

I could hear Mum and Dad talking on the phone downstairs, discussing something that I couldn't quite make out.

I stood up and went over to the window, and after fiddling the latch open, I flung the window out as wide as it could go, so I could feel the fresh air stream in around me. The garden lay still and peaceful below, lit up by the soft evening light.

"I want to go home," I spoke out loud. "I don't want to be here."

As though I had commanded it, a fourth hole split open just outside the window.

Just as before, the black lines whirled and eddied in rhythm only with each other.

I could hear my other mum and dad saying goodbye to the person on the phone and the sound of their taut laughter. In the next moment, they would come back upstairs to find me.

For a few seconds, I paused. If I stayed here, I wouldn't have to live with having asthma and my family wouldn't either. I could probably get along with this other mum and dad, although they weren't around as much as my real mum and dad were. Perhaps I could even be friends with the Rav in this world too, I wouldn't have to be friends just with Mandy. I could feel all of this stretching out in front of me, like a road I'd not travelled down before. The hole seemed to turn in a circle in that moment, neither growing larger or smaller but just rotating round and round.

I looked over my shoulder at the huge room that my other parents were working so hard to get for me, because they thought it was what I really wanted. In this place, somehow, we'd lost sight of what was really important.

The hole started to slow and then it began to shrink. I let all that I had learned wash over me before I leaped towards the hole, into the black lines, until they surrounded me and all I could see was them.

Right Here

I opened my eyes.

I was back on the sofa.

Mum and Dad were rushing towards me with a bag packed for hospital and my inhalers.

Only moments had passed while I'd been gone.

Back here, I could feel the closed feeling grip around my lungs again. I wheezed painfully but then Mum and Dad were beside me with my nebulizer.

"Nice and slow, my love," Dad said.

"Deep breath," said Mum.

I reached towards them and felt their arms warm around me. It was all I wanted.

And I never saw a hole again.

READING ZONE!

TOP READING TIP

Books can take you on fantastic adventures from the comfort of wherever you are.

As you are reading, you can imagine the places in the story so you feel as if you are there.

As a reader, you will automatically add your own ideas to the author's descriptions so you have a vivid picture of the setting.

READING ZONE!

WHAT DO YOU THINK?

When Mae had gone through
the hole and had a new life,
how did you feel for her?

Did you think she would be able
to come back to her real life?

What would you have done –
are there things you wish were
different about your life?

READING ZONE!

QUIZ TIME

Can you remember the answers to these questions?

- What is the first thing Mae says she does when she gets home from hospital?

- When did Rav and Mae first become friends in Mae's normal life?

- How long does Mandy tell Mae they have been friends for?

- Why is Mae's mum surprised that Mae is not more excited about moving house?

READING ZONE!

STORYTELLING TOOLKIT

There are a lot of conversations between the characters in this story.

The author uses them to help us to understand what is going on, and what the characters think and feel.

Why not have a go at writing your own conversation between you and a friend?

You'll need to use speech punctuation to signal to the reader the actual words that are spoken.